SEE ME PLAY

I Like to Read® books, created by award-winning
picture book artists as well as talented newcomers,
instill confidence and the joy of reading in new readers.

We want to hear every new reader say, "I like to read!"

Visit our website for flash cards, activities, and more about the series:
www.holidayhouse.com/ILiketoRead
#ILTR

This book has been officially leveled by using the
F&P Text Level Gradient™ Leveling System.

SEE ME PLAY

Paul Meisel

I Like to Read®

HOLIDAY HOUSE • NEW YORK

I LIKE TO READ is a registered trademark of Holiday House Publishing, Inc.
Copyright © 2019 by Paul Meisel
All Rights Reserved
HOLIDAY HOUSE is registered in the U.S. Patent and Trademark Office.
Printed and bound in August 2020 at Tien Wah Press, Johor Bahru, Johor, Malaysia.
Artwork was created with pen and ink with watercolor and acrylic on Strathmore paper and digital tools.
www.holidayhouse.com
First Edition
3 5 7 9 10 8 6 4 2

This book has been officially leveled by using the F&P Text Level Gradient™ Leveling System.

Library of Congress Cataloging-in-Publication Data
Names: Meisel, Paul, author, illustrator.
Title: See me play / Paul Meisel.
Description: First edition. | New York : Holiday House, [2019] | Series:
I like to read | Summary: In this easy-to-read book, a playful pack of dogs
chase a ball that is caught by a bird, a whale, and a lion.
Identifiers: LCCN 2018024183 | ISBN 9780823438327 (hardcover)
Subjects: | CYAC: Play—Fiction. | Dogs—Fiction. | Animals—Fiction.
Classification: LCC PZ7.M5158752 Sdv 2019 | DDC [E]—dc23 LC record available at https://lccn.loc.gov/2018024183

ISBN: 978-0-8234-3835-8 (paperback)

FOR PETE AND LIZ—AND RILEY!

I see the ball.

I see the ball.

The ball is fast.

The ball is wet.

The bird wants the ball.

The bird has the ball.

The bird drops the ball.

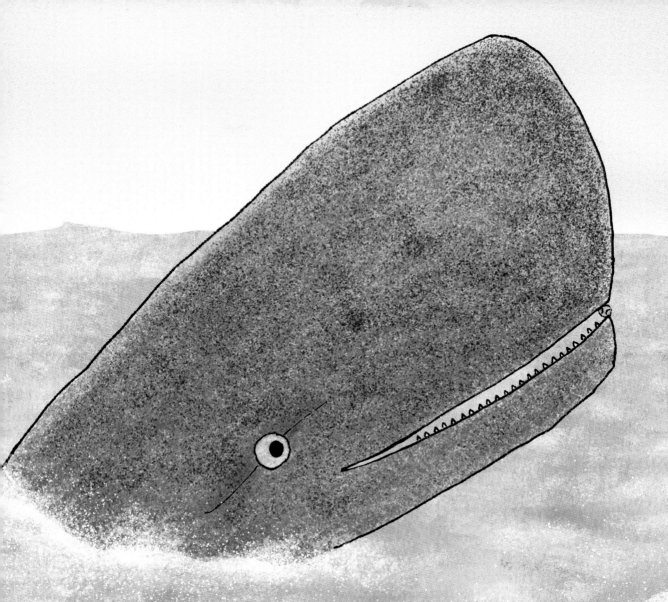

The whale has the ball.

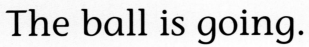

The ball is going.

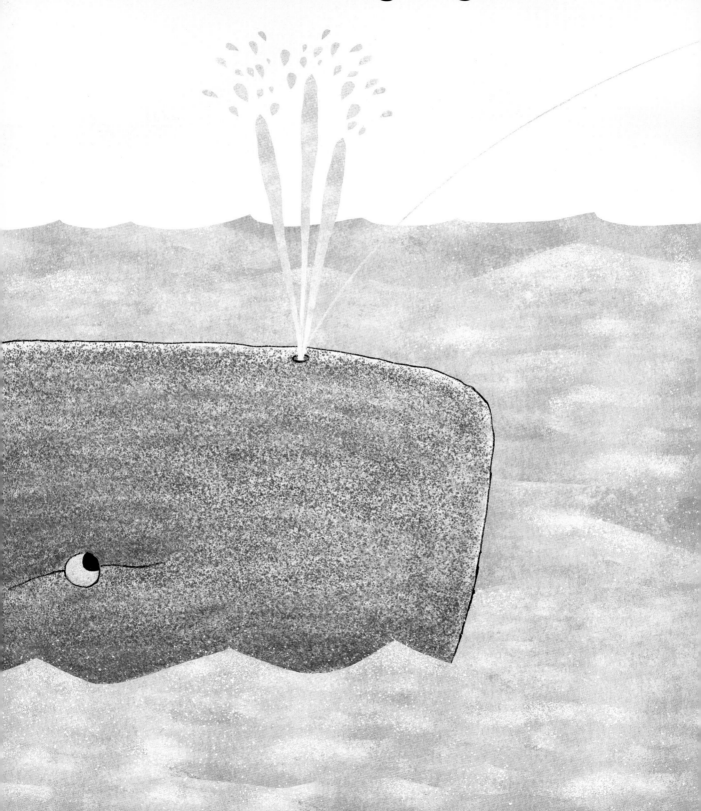

The lion has the ball.

The ball is gone.

Gulp!

I see a stick.

Also by Paul Meisel

I Like to Read®

Theodor Seuss Geisel
Honor Award

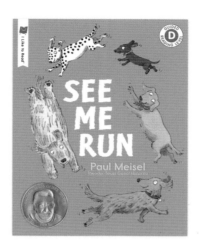

Theodor Seuss Geisel
Honor Award

Kirkus Reviews Best Book

A NATURE DIARY

AAAS (American Association for the
Advancement of Science)/Subaru
Excellence in Children's Books Finalist

Cooperative Children's Book Center (CCBC)
Best-of-the-Year List

Science Best Books for Curious Kids

Virginia Readers' Choices

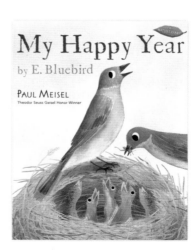

A Junior Library Guild Selection